P9-ELG-323

CH

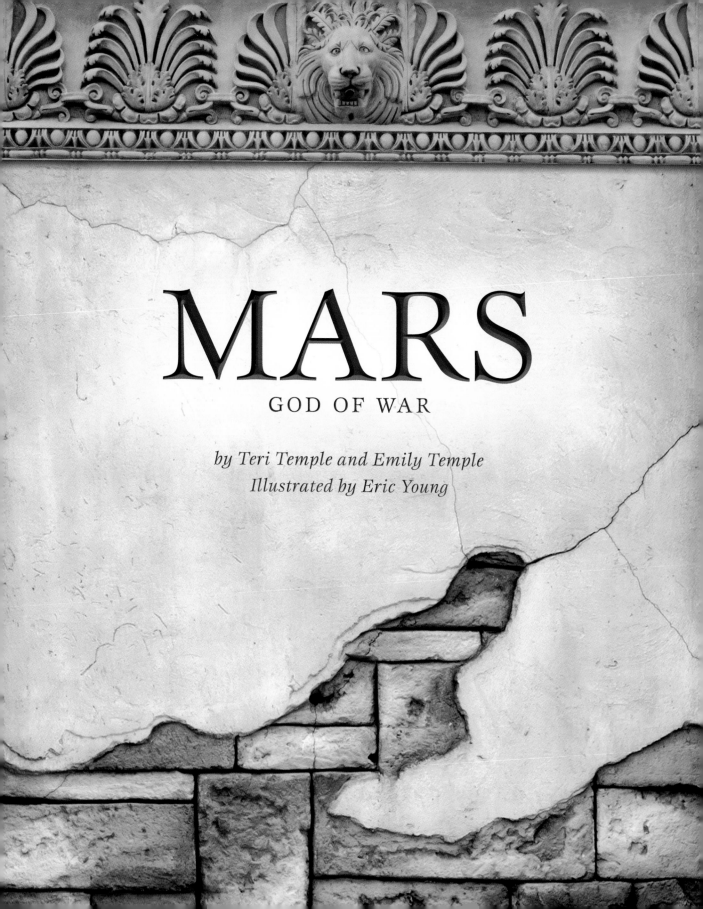

MARS

GOD OF WAR

by Teri Temple and Emily Temple

Illustrated by Eric Young

The Child's World

Published by The Child's World®
1980 Lookout Drive • Mankato, MN 56003-1705
800-599-READ • www.childsworld.com

ACKNOWLEDGMENTS
The Child's World®: Mary Berendes, Publishing Director
Red Line Editorial: Editorial direction
The Design Lab: Design and production
Design elements ©: Banana Republic Images/Shutterstock Images; Shutterstock
Images; Anton Balazh/Shutterstock Images
Photographs ©: Viacheslav Lopatin/Shutterstock Images, 5; Thinkstock, 11;
Shutterstock Images, 12, 18, 23, 28

ISBN 9781631437199
LCCN 2014945437

Printed in the United States of America
Mankato, MN
November, 2014
PA02241

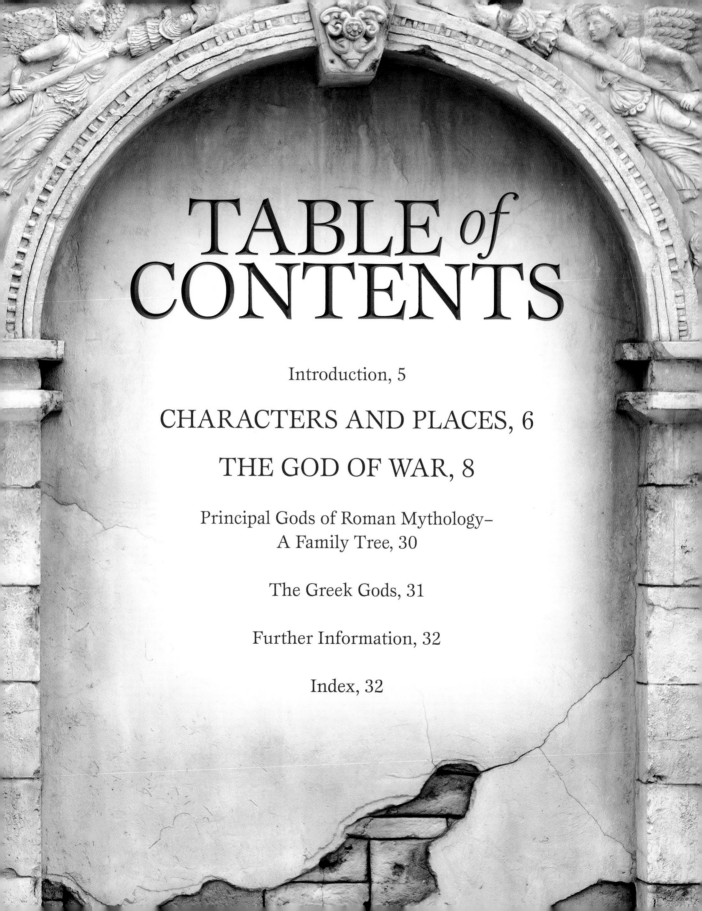

TABLE *of* CONTENTS

INTRODUCTION

In ancient times Romans believed in spirits or gods called numina. In Latin, *numina* means divine will or power. The Romans took part in religious rituals to please the gods. They felt the gods had powers that could make their lives better.

As the Roman government grew more powerful, its armies conquered many neighboring lands. Romans often adopted beliefs from these new cultures. They greatly admired the Greek arts and sciences. Gradually, the Romans combined the Greek myths and religion with their own. These stories shaped and influenced each part of a Roman citizen's daily life. Ancient Roman poets, such as Ovid and Virgil, wrote down these tales of wonder. Their writings became a part of Rome's great history. To the Romans, however, these stories were not just for entertainment. Roman mythology was their key to understanding the world.

ANCIENT ROMAN SOCIETIES

Ancient Roman society was divided into several groups. The patricians were the most powerful and wealthiest group. They often owned land and held power in the government. The plebeians worked for the patricians. Slaves were prisoners of war or children without parents. Some slaves were freed and enjoyed most of the rights of citizens.

CHARACTERS AND PLACES

ANCIENT ROME

ADRIATIC SEA

ROME

TYRRHENIAN SEA

TROJAN WAR: *War between the ancient Greeks and Trojans*

ANNA PERENNA
(an-NUH PUR-en-nuh)

Main character in Roman myth about Mars

BELLONA (buh-LOH-nuh)

Ancient Roman goddess of war; attendant of Mars

DIOMEDES
(dahy-uh-MEE-deez)

Greek hero of the Trojan War; son of Mars

DISCORDIA
(dis-KAWR-dee-uh)

Goddess of discord and strife; attendant of Mars

JUNO *(JOO-noh)*

Queen of the gods; married to Jupiter

MARS *(MAHRZ)*

God of war; son of Jupiter and Juno; possible father of Cupid

MERCURY *(MUR-kyuh-ree)*

Messenger to the gods; god of trade; son of Jupiter

METUS *(MEHT-us)*

God of terror; son and attendant of Mars

MINERVA *(mi-NUR-vuh)*

Goddess of wisdom and the arts; daughter of Jupiter

OTUS AND EPHIALTES
(OH-tuhs and *eff-ee-ALL-tees)*

Twin giants; sons of Neptune

REMUS *(REE-muhs)*

Twin brother to Romulus; killed by his brother when trying to create Rome; son of Mars

ROMULUS *(ROM-yuh-luhs)*

Founder of Rome and its first king; twin brother to Remus; son of Mars

TIMOR *(TEE-mawr)*

God of fear; son and attendant of Mars

VENUS *(VEE-nuhs)*

Goddess of love and beauty; born of sea foam; wife of Vulcan; mother of Cupid

VULCAN *(VULH-kuhn)*

God of fire and metalwork; son of Jupiter and Juno; married to Venus

THE GOD OF WAR

Mars was one of the most commonly worshipped gods in ancient Roman times. The story of his birth is anything but ordinary. Hidden high in the clouds was a marvelous golden palace called Mount Olympus. It was home to the Olympic gods. Originally there were three brothers, Neptune, Pluto, and Jupiter. There were also three sisters, Ceres, Vesta, and Juno. The six gods ruled over the heavens and the earth.

Jupiter and Juno were king and queen of the gods. Jupiter was not faithful to his wife. Juno was jealous that Jupiter had produced a child, Minerva, without her. Juno decided to get revenge by having a child of her own, Mars. She asked the goddess of flowers and blossoming plants, Flora, to help her. Flora touched Juno with a magical herb that made her pregnant with Mars. When the gods found out Juno was pregnant, they were excited. However, Juno was still angry with Jupiter. She passed that anger onto Mars. He was born with a violent personality that kept most other gods away.

The earliest Romans worshipped Mars as a god of spring, fertility, and the protector of cattle. Mars was considered a gentle god who encouraged farming. Romans started thinking of him as their protector. They called him the father of their city. Mars was second only to Jupiter in importance among the gods. As Mars was compared more to the Greek god Ares, Mars started to serve as the god of war.

The Romans called Mars *Gradivus* because of his warlike steps to the battlefield. They believed Mars marched before them to battle, acting as their invisible protector. As the god of farming, he was called *Silvanus*. When Mars was guardian of the state, Romans called him *Quirinus*.

Mars was the perfect representation of manliness. Ancient Romans pictured him as youthful, tall, and muscular. His body combined great strength and agility. In art, Mars always appeared ready for battle. He was shown wearing a helmet and carrying a sword and spear. Even as the god of war, Mars still looked after farming. He was a god of protection who looked over the state.

JANUS

Some scholars consider Janus the god of all beginnings. He protected Rome as well as Mars during battle. A janus was a ceremonial gateway. The freestanding structures were symbols for successful entrances or exits. There were many lucky and unlucky ways to march through a janus. The Roman army marched through these gates. The most famous shrine was the Janus Geminus. The doors were traditionally kept open in times of war and closed when Rome was at peace.

Eventually the Romans adopted the myths and culture of the ancient Greeks. When the Roman and Greek stories combined, Mars lost his calm nature.

Mars was well liked and honored. As the god of war, Mars was a fierce warrior. He was strong and fast. He often started fights. Even though he was ferocious in battle, Mars only liked to start a war if there was a good reason. This was different from Ares, who thrived on endless fighting. Mars was also better at using strategy in war. He became an expert in all areas of warfare.

ARES

Ares was the Greek god of war. The Greeks told a different story of the god's birth. His parents were Zeus and Hera, the king and queen of the world of ancient Greek gods. Ares was tall and handsome, but he was mean and self-centered. He was disliked by most of the gods. When ancient Greeks went to war, Ares was the first to get involved. He did not care who won or lost; he just liked battle and bloodshed.

Mars had two half siblings named Juventas and Vulcan. They shared a mother with Juno. Juventas was the goddess of youth. Vulcan was the god of fire. Mars never got along with his siblings, but he was most frustrated by Minerva, his half sister. Minerva was the goddess of wisdom and arts. Minerva was also a goddess of war. She was Mars's enemy. The half siblings represented the two sides of war. Mars preferred to fight using muscles and force. Minerva represented the intellectual and strategic side of war.

Because Mars was so closely linked to the Greek god Ares, there is only one story about him that is distinctly Roman. This story tells of Mars and Anna Perenna. Anna Perenna was Minerva's assistant. Mars developed a passion for his sister Minerva, even though she frustrated him. He selected Anna Perenna to help him marry Minerva. Anna Perenna was older and wiser than Minerva. She understood quickly that Minerva would never give in to Mars's charms, so she came up with a plan. Mars was to visit Minerva and marry her by force.

When he arrived, he was shocked to see that instead of Minerva, Anna Perenna was dressed to be his bride. Anna had fooled Mars and ruined his plans to wed Minerva.

While Mars had many affairs, he had only one true love. His heart belonged to the goddess of love, Venus. It was love at first sight when Mars set eyes on the beautiful goddess. He had an opportunity to marry Venus, but his brother, Vulcan, ruined his chances. After Juno tried to lead a rebellion against Jupiter, Jupiter had his wife imprisoned. Juno promised that whoever could free her could have Venus's hand in marriage. Mars tried and failed. So he asked Vulcan for help. Instead of helping Mars, Vulcan freed Juno and claimed Venus for himself.

Venus did not like Vulcan, who was ugly and deformed. She preferred the strong and handsome Mars. Venus and Mars secretly met. They thought they could outsmart Vulcan. But Vulcan learned of their affair from Sol, the Sun god. Vulcan set a trap to catch them. Vulcan was a master blacksmith and craftsman. He created a magical net. Then he had Sol watch for Mars and Venus.

When Sol caught Venus and Mars, Vulcan planned to embarrass them into ending their relationship. When the couple awoke, they were faced with all of the gods and goddesses waiting to pass judgment. Unfortunately for Vulcan, the gods agreed that Mars and Venus belonged together. However, Venus was forced to stay married to Vulcan.

Although Venus was Mars's true love, she was not his only love. His strength and manliness caught the eye of many maidens.

Mars was never married, but he had many children, both mortal and immortal. Many of his children also had aggressive, warlike personalities. Mars's son Diomedes was ferocious in battle. He was a Greek hero. He even wounded his own father during the Trojan War. Mars was also the father of two Amazon warrior queens.

Venus and Mars had three sons and one daughter together. Their older sons, Timor and Metus, were constant companions to Mars on the battlefield. Metus was the god of terror. Timor was the god of fear. Their daughter, Concordia, was Mars's complete opposite. She became

AMAZONS

The Amazons were a race of warrior women. Men were not allowed to be part of the Amazons' families. Mars was allowed to support the Amazons and their wars. Mars also had a special connection to the Amazons. They worshipped Mars as the father of their tribe. He was the father of two of their most famous queens, Penthesilia and Hippolte.

the lovely goddess of harmony. Some stories say Venus
and Mars had another son named Cupid. He was the
mischievous god of love.

Mars spent a lot of time traveling to seek out and start wars. He rode in a chariot pulled by horses. It made quite an impression when he rode into battle. Bellona, a goddess of war, drove the chariot. She was Mars's female counterpart and constant companion. While driving, she held up a flaming torch to light the way for Mars's followers.

Though he was not well liked by the other gods, Mars was the most prominent military god in the Roman army. Soldiers were loyal to him. On the battlefield, they gladly followed him to their deaths. His closest companions were his sons Metus and Timor. They enjoyed helping their father create chaos and confusion on battlefields.

Another loyal follower of Mars was Discordia. She was the goddess of strife. Discordia owned a magical golden apple. This apple caused the Trojan War to break out. Discordia would lead the way into war alongside Mars and his companions.

One of ancient history's fiercest wars involved Mars
and one of his children. The Trojan War was an epic battle
fought between the ancient Greeks and the city of Troy.
It began over the kidnapping of a Greek queen. It seemed
all of the Olympic gods had an interest in this war. Venus

wanted to help the handsome Trojan prince Paris. Mars had promised his mother, Juno, that he would support the Greeks. But Venus convinced Mars to switch sides.

This meant Mars joined Venus, Apollo, and Diana on the side of the people of Troy. Minerva, Juno, Neptune, Mercury, and Vulcan sided with Greece. These gods held grudges against the Trojans. During the battle, Mars found himself fighting his own son, the Greek hero Diomedes. Diomedes injured Mars with his spear.

Mars left the field roaring like 10,000 bulls. Venus rushed to be with him, but she was also injured. They both survived and eventually made it back to Mount Olympus. Mars complained to Jupiter that he had been mistreated. Jupiter did not care and would not fix the problem. Mars would not be able to fight the rest of the Trojan War.

ROMAN LEGION

The Roman army was made up of approximately 28 legions. Each legion had an estimated 4,800 soldiers. The Roman army was very organized and successful. Most soldiers were men from the plebeian, or poor, class. They were required to be at least 20 years old and Roman citizens. Their armor was made of strips of iron and leather. It included a metal helmet and a curved shield to protect their body.

Mars rarely spent time off the battlefield. But the Aloadae Giants held Mars captive for 13 months. The Aloadae Giants were twin brothers so strong they gave the gods trouble. Their names were Otus and Ephialtes. They believed they were great enough to take over Mount Olympus. Mars tried to stop them, but even he was defeated. They chained Mars, sealed him in a jar, and left him.

For 13 months Mars tried to free himself. Finally, when he became too weak to continue, the stepmother of the giants, Eeriboia, felt bad. She told Mercury, the messenger god, of Mars's trouble. Mercury was the fastest god. He snuck in and stole Mars from the giants. Mercury returned Mars to Mount Olympus. Mars spent many days recovering his strength. It was a humiliating experience for the god of war.

The most famous myth involving Mars also included a set of twins. Romulus and Remus were twin boys born to a princess named Rhea Silvia. Mars was their father. The king where they lived did not want any heirs to the throne. To prevent them from taking his throne, he left them in the Tiber River. The king figured they would not survive long. A she-wolf and a woodpecker found them and protected them from wild animals. Then a shepherd came across the boys. He took them home to raise them as his own.

As Romulus and Remus grew older, they became natural leaders like their father. One day Remus was captured and taken to the king, where his true identity was revealed. Romulus ran to his brother's rescue, killing the king in the process. The people of the city offered them the crown. They turned it down in order to start a city of their own. They came to the place where Rome is located today. They waited for a sign from the gods. Remus saw a sign of six vultures, but Romulus saw 12. The brothers fought over whose sign was the correct one. In his rage, Romulus killed Remus. Romulus continued to

work on the city. According to legend, he founded Rome
in 753 BC, making himself king and giving the city his
name. It was one of the most powerful cities in the world
for more than 1,000 years.

Since Mars was the father of Romulus and Remus, the legendary founders of Rome, he was also considered the father of the Roman people. They thought of themselves as children of Mars. Mars had two main sanctuaries of worship in Rome. The first was the temple of Mars Gradivus. It was a shared temple with Jupiter and Quirinus, located on the Capitol. The Roman army would gather there before they went to war. The second temple was the Mars Ultor. It was located on the Forum of Augustus.

WHAT'S IN A NAME?
Mars was one of the most popular gods. As such, many things were given his name. The fourth planet from the sun is called Mars. It is the second smallest in the solar system. Because the planet is a blood red color, the Romans named it after the god of war. The month of March was also named to honor Mars. March was the month when wars would begin or start again. In ancient Rome, Tuesday was also known as the "Day of Mars." They called it *Dies Marti*.

The Campus Martius was also dedicated to Mars. It was a large field outside the city where army members and athletes trained.

The Roman people held several festivals in Mars's honor each year. On March 1, they asked him to keep enemies away from their crops and herds. Another festival on October 19 purified the weapons of soldiers. Mars was a special combination of the gentle god of spring and nature's growth and the god of war. He was worshipped and loved by the people as their protector. Though he fought with siblings and mortals, he has a unique place in the myths and stories of the ancient Roman people.

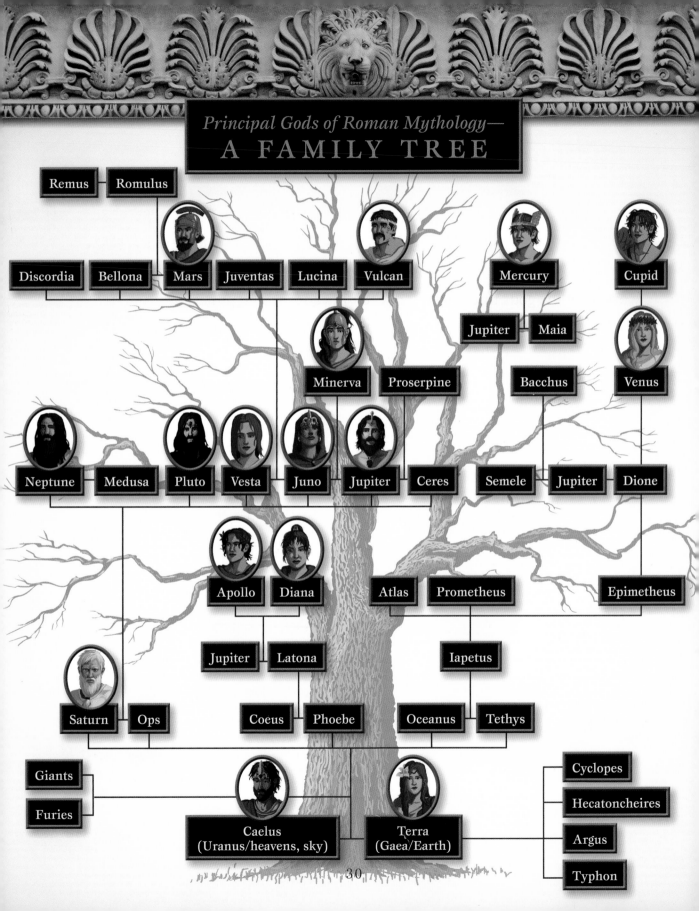

Principal Gods of Roman Mythology—
A FAMILY TREE

Remus — Romulus

Discordia — Bellona — Mars — Juventas — Lucina — Vulcan

Mercury

Cupid

Minerva — Proserpine

Jupiter — Maia

Bacchus

Venus

Neptune — Medusa — Pluto — Vesta — Juno — Jupiter — Ceres

Semele — Jupiter — Dione

Apollo — Diana

Atlas — Prometheus

Epimetheus

Jupiter — Latona

Iapetus

Saturn — Ops

Coeus — Phoebe

Oceanus — Tethys

Giants

Furies

Caelus
(Uranus/heavens, sky)

Terra
(Gaea/Earth)

Cyclopes

Hecatoncheires

Argus

Typhon

THE GREEK GODS

Ancient Greeks believed gods and goddesses ruled the world. The gods fell in love and struggled for power, but they never died. The ancient Greeks believed their gods were immortal. The Greek people worshiped the gods in temples. They felt the gods would protect and guide them. Over time, the Romans and many other cultures adopted the Greek myths as their own. While these other cultures changed the names of the gods, many of the stories remain the same.

SATURN: *Cronus*
God of Time and God of Sowing
Symbol: Sickle or Scythe

JUPITER: *Zeus*
King of the Gods, God of Sky, Rain, and Thunder
Symbols: Thunderbolt, Eagle, and Oak Tree

JUNO: *Hera*
Queen of the Gods, Goddess of Marriage,
*   Pregnancy, and Childbirth*
Symbols: Peacock, Cow, and Diadem
*   (Diamond Crown)*

NEPTUNE: *Poseidon*
God of the Sea
Symbols: Trident, Horse, and Dolphin

PLUTO: *Hades*
God of the Underworld
Symbols: Invisibility Helmet and Pomegranate

MINERVA: *Athena*
Goddess of Wisdom, War, and Arts and Crafts
Symbols: Owl, Shield, Loom, and Olive Tree

MARS: *Ares*
God of War
Symbols: Wild Boar, Vulture, and Dog

DIANA: *Artemis*
Goddess of the Moon and Hunt
Symbols: Deer, Moon, and Silver Bow and Arrows

APOLLO: *Apollo*
God of the Sun, Music, Healing, and Prophecy
Symbols: Laurel Tree, Lyre, Bow, and Raven

VENUS: *Aphrodite*
Goddess of Love and Beauty
Symbols: Dove, Swan, and Rose

CUPID: *Eros*
God of Love
Symbols: Bow and Arrows

MERCURY: *Hermes*
Messenger to the Gods, God of Travelers and Trade
Symbols: Crane, Caduceus, Winged Sandals,
*   and Helmet*

FURTHER INFORMATION

BOOKS

Johnson, Robin. *Understanding Roman Myths*. New York: Crabtree Publishing, 2012.

Temple, Teri. *Ares: God of War*. Mankato, MN: Child's World, 2013.

WEB SITES

Visit our Web site for links about Mars: *childsworld.com/links*

Note to Parents, Teachers, and Librarians: We routinely verify our Web links to make sure they are safe and active sites. So encourage your readers to check them out!

INDEX